THE THREE
AND MANY WISHES
OF JASON REID

HAZEL HUTCHINS

THE THREE
AND MANY WISHES
OF JASON REID

Illustrated by Julie Tennent

VIKING KESTREL

VIKING KESTREL
Viking Penguin Inc., 40 West 23rd Street, New York, New York 10010, U.S.A.
Penguin Books Ltd, 27 Wrights Lane, London W8 5TZ (Publishing & Editorial) and
Harmondsworth, Middlesex, England (Distribution & Warehouse)
Penguin Books Australia Ltd, Ringwood, Victoria, Australia
Penguin Books Canada Limited, 2801 John Street, Markham, Ontario, Canada L3R 1B4
Penguin Books (N.Z.) Ltd, 182–190 Wairau Road, Auckland 10, New Zealand

First published in Canada by Annick Press Ltd., 1983
This edition with illustrations by Julie Tennent first published in
Great Britain by Penguin Books Ltd, 1987
First American edition published by Viking Penguin Inc., 1988
Text copyright © H. J. Hutchins, 1983
Illustrations copyright © Julie Tennent, 1987
All rights reserved
Printed in the United States of America by Arcata Graphics, Fairfield, Pennsylvania
Set in Garamond Book
1   2   3   4   5   92   91   90   89   88

Library of Congress Cataloging-in-Publication Data
Wilson, Hazel Hutchins
The three and many wishes of Jason Reid / by Hazel Hutchins;
illustrated by Julie Tennent—1st American ed.
p. cm.
Summary: Eleven-year-old Jason is granted three wishes which land
him and his friends in some hilarious scrapes.
ISBN 0-670-82155-1
[1. Wishes—Fiction.   2. Humorous stories.]   I. Tennent, Julie,
ill.   II. Title   PZ7.W695Ti   1988   [E]   dc19   87-24153   I. Title.

THE THREE
AND MANY WISHES
OF JASON REID

Jason Reid was eleven years old when he met the Elster of the Third Order, 'Quicksilver' by name. It happened in the back alley of Fourth Street on a hot June afternoon. Jason was walking home from school. Quicksilver was sitting on an upside-down dustbin.

'Hello Jason,' said Quicksilver. 'I'm glad to see you today. I was here yesterday but you didn't come by when you should have.'

Jason pulled his cap down low over his eyes.

'Baseball practice,' he said, squinting out from beneath the visor.

'They forgot to tell me about that,' said Quicksilver with a frown. Then he shrugged and smiled in a matter-of-fact manner. 'Oh well. You have three wishes. What will it be?'

Now Jason had not been alive eleven years for nothing. He knew many things. He knew, for example, that eleven-year-old boys should not stop in back alleys to talk to strangers. It was, as his father said, a good way to get into a lot of trouble.

This stranger, however, was no more than eighteen inches high. His hands were the size of the knobs on Jason's dresser drawers at home. His feet were like the long fat ju-jubes that Jason liked to buy at the corner store. His face, more lined than Jason's dad's face but younger than his grandmother's, had a look on it that clearly said he expected Jason to stay exactly where he was. And, even more important, although Jason did indeed try to run away, he found that his own feet were stuck very firmly to the ground.

'Why me?' asked Jason.

'Why not?' said Quicksilver.

'Who are you?' asked Jason.

'Roughly translated – I think "Quicksilver" will do nicely for my name. I am an Elster of the Third Order. I am stepping through.' Quicksilver said this rather formally. Then he frowned at Jason. 'According to the pact that's all I'm required to tell you. Are you going to wish or not?'

Jason tugged his cap down even lower over

his eyes. He tilted his head back, so he could still see out from beneath it.

'Three wishes?' he asked.

'Three wishes,' replied Quicksilver.

'I'd like a new baseball glove,' said Jason. 'I'd like a baseball glove that is my size exactly and magic too, so that any ball I wanted to catch I could catch. That's wish number one.'

Quicksilver smiled.

'Granted,' he said.

Jason felt a slight weight at the end of his left arm. He looked down. There on his hand he saw a most wonderful baseball glove. It looked and felt as soft as velvet. It smelled wonderfully of the finest leather. It fit exactly to Jason's hand.

'Number two?' asked Quicksilver.

'I . . . I . . . I . . . I . . . I . . . I . . . I . . . I . . .,' said Jason.

'Think first,' said Quicksilver. 'Think it out first. Then speak it aloud. It works better that way.'

Jason clamped his mouth shut. He was a very good thinker. In fact, a good deal more hard thinking went on beneath Jason's baseball cap than most people suspected. His mind began to work at a furious pace. He was desperately trying to remember all the stories he had ever heard or read about magical beings and wishes. He knew the stories always ended badly. The people in them quickly became greedy and careless and wasted their wishes on the smallest and meanest of things. That was total foolishness, as far as Jason was concerned.

Why, just standing there in the back alley of Fourth Street, Jason could think of at least ten good, solid, worthwhile and special wishes. No one ever offered to grant ten wishes, of course. The offer was always only good for three. Then Jason remembered the trace of an idea he had had a long time ago. It had seemed a good idea then. It seemed like an even better idea now.

Jason glanced down again at the glove. Oh, but it really was a wonderful glove. He wanted very, very badly to try it out. Suddenly, no matter what other plans were forming in his mind, he knew he simply could not bear to lose that glove.

'Can you make it so that everyone will accept the glove without asking where it came from?' asked Jason. 'I don't want anyone, especially not Mom and Dad and the police to think I stole it. I just want to be able to use it as long as I want to without anyone having a fit about it. I want everyone to think it's a perfectly normal glove. Could you do that?'

'Yes,' said Quicksilver.

'OK,' said Jason. 'That's wish number two.'

Quicksilver drew his eyebrows together. He set his eyes intently on a spot just beyond Jason's left shoulder. There was a soft, hollow sound like the wind blowing through a long pipe. Quicksilver looked back at Jason.

'Granted,' he said. 'Number three?'

Jason knew what he wanted to wish for next. His heart was racing like a train barrelling downhill. Did he dare? Did he dare?

He closed his eyes. Very quickly and in a very small voice he said, 'I wish for three more wishes.'

There was complete silence. Now I've done it, thought Jason. Now I've lost him altogether.

Slowly Jason opened his eyes. To his surprise Quicksilver was still there. There was a confident look on his face.

'You can't have any more wishes,' he said simply. 'Three. That's it.'

'Why?' asked Jason.

'Those are the rules,' said Quicksilver.

'What rules?' asked Jason.

'These rules,' answered Quicksilver. 'Only a field guide, of course, but it's all clearly in here.'

From his jacket he took a small blue book and a pair of wire-rimmed glasses. He put on the glasses, opened the book and read aloud.

'Wishes to be granted – not four, or five, or ten at a time – but three at a time, no matter how the candidate asks or what he offers in return.' Quicksilver closed the book and looked at Jason. 'Now, wish.'

'I just did,' said Jason stubbornly. 'I'm not asking for more wishes. I'm *wishing* for more wishes. Three at a time. Just the way the book says.'

Quicksilver shook his head. He stood up, tucked the book and glasses back into his pocket and brushed off his clothes.

'Well, that's that then. You're clearly breaking the pact. I shouldn't have any trouble getting through at all now.' And he disappeared.

Jason stood alone in the middle of the alley. He had the oddest feeling about him. It was not a feeling of surprise, which would have been natural, but the strangest feeling that something was not quite finished. He looked down at his glove and then across at the dustbin again.

Quicksilver was back. There was a very, very puzzled look on his face.

'It's still shut,' he said.

'What's shut?' asked Jason from beneath his baseball cap.

'The way through,' said Quicksilver, with obvious annoyance. He was staring so hard at Jason that Jason began to feel extremely uncomfortable.

'I don't understand,' said Jason.

'Neither do I,' said Quicksilver. 'Every angle is supposed to be covered. It's always been covered before. There aren't supposed to be any loopholes.' He shook his head and frowned. 'Apparently, however, you've found one.'

'Does that mean I get my third wish after all?' asked Jason, barely daring to hope.

Quicksilver nodded abruptly.

'Not immediately,' he said. 'Three at a time means we'll have to wait a day or two.'

'Saturday,' said Jason quickly, before the other

13

could change his mind. 'After the baseball game. I'll meet you at the west end of the park on Poplar Street. Wait in the little ring of bushes under the cottonwood tree.'

'Very well,' said Quicksilver. And then he disappeared.

2

Spider Wellman was the pitcher on Jason's baseball team. They called him Spider because he looked like a spider. His arms and legs were long, long, long. Spider had such long arms and legs

that Jason often wondered how he could control them. But control them he did. Spider Wellman had better control of his arms and legs than anyone else on the team. Spider Wellman caught pop flys and foul balls with the deft outreaching of his mitt. And when he came to bat, Spider Wellman never struck out.

'It's not enough just to keep your eye on the ball,' Spider told Jason as they waited for the Saturday game to start. 'You've got to keep your mind on the ball too. Don't go thinking about how great it'll be if you catch it or how awful it'll be if you miss. Just think about getting underneath it.'

'You're wasting your time, Spider,' cut in Oakly Barnes. 'He's hopeless. Even if a fly ball landed in Jason's glove, he'd be sure to drop it.'

It was quite true. Several balls had been actually known to land in Jason's old mitt only to mysteriously escape out the back end. Somehow.

'Lay off, Oakly,' called Penny from where she was carefully weighing a baseball bat between the fingertips of her right hand. Her friendly round face with its frame of brown hair looked across at them speculatively. 'Jason might not be as bad as we thought. I was helping him practise last night and he caught everything in sight. It was strange how he did it sometimes, but he did.'

Jason couldn't quite meet Penny's look. He had badly wanted to explain everything to Penny last night. He had especially wanted to explain when the glove had lifted him four feet into the air to catch a wild ball, but frankly, Jason hadn't known quite what to say. All he knew was that his mind had been doing a lot of thinking over the past two days, and beneath it all a plan was forming. It was a plan so big and so grand that Jason could hardly believe it himself. It was a wonderful plan.

'I'll believe it when I see it,' said Oakly. 'As far as I'm concerned, he's a wash-out.' He stepped on Jason's toe, not quite by accident, as he went over with Spider for the coin toss.

'Sometimes I could just cream that Oakly,' said Penny. She dropped the bat, hiked one foot up on the bench, and retied a well worn shoelace.

'How come he doesn't ever get you going, Jason?' she asked.

'He's just Oakly,' said Jason, matter-of-factly.

'And you're "just Jason",' said Penny, giving him an odd little look. Penny did not believe in being 'just' anything. Then she broke into a grin. 'I sure hope you're still catching them like you were last night.'

'I hope so too,' said Jason. 'I only wi . . .' He choked the words off quickly.

'What?' asked Penny.

'Nothing,' said Jason in a loud, firm voice, 'I didn't say anything about wishing for anything. I was going to say something entirely different.'

'All right, all right. Don't shout my head off,' said Penny. 'Let's go! We're out in field.'

Jason jogged with Penny to her position at second base. He watched thoughtfully as she kicked the bag three times and walked clockwise around it the way she always did. It was a tried and tested ritual with her. Penny wasn't superstitious. She believed she could do almost anything if she tried hard enough – but she always gave herself every possible advantage just in case.

'Penny, if you had three wishes, what would you wish for?' asked Jason.

'Jason, think about the game. Don't think

about something weird. Think about the game,' she replied, giving the base a final thump.

'I just want to know,' pressed Jason. 'What would you wish for in three wishes?'

'I don't know,' said Penny. 'There's big wishes and there's little wishes and will you please get out in left field where you belong! And remember what Spider said. Keep your eye and everything else on the ball!'

Jason jogged across to left field. He knew what Penny meant. There were little wishes and big wishes. Jason's magic glove had been a little wish. The pot of gold that one of the poor old couples had wished for in one of the stories he had read – well, that had been a little wish too. But what Jason had in mind today – once he was certain the glove really worked and the magic was real – what Jason had in mind was truly grand.

'Jason!' It was Penny's voice calling urgently from across the field. 'Jason, get it!'

He had been dreaming again, Jason knew. He had been out in left field dreaming. He didn't even know where the ball was, except that it wasn't on the ground, so it must be up in the sky somewhere.

Glove, catch the ball. Catch the ball, thought Jason, exactly as he had learned to do while practising the night before. There was a jerk at the end of his hand. Jason was bounced on to the balls of his feet and then the glove pulled him running across the field. He could see the ball now. It was whirling hard towards him. It was coming so fast and so sudden that he wanted to duck. But the glove wouldn't let him. The glove held his whole body ready and poised, waiting, straining for the ball.

Thunk.

The sweetest sound in the world, thought Jason, is when a high fly lands perfectly in an outfielder's glove.

'Way to go!' called Penny.

'About time!' came Oakly's voice from first.

Spider Wellman wiped his nose on his sleeve and easily caught the ball that Penny relayed in to him. Spider said nothing. Spider was going to be a pro ball player for the Expos one day. Nothing broke Spider's concentration. But Jason knew by the way he slipped his cap on and off his head several times that he, too, was pleased.

Five times that afternoon Jason caught fly balls. Low flys, high flys, balls that lost themselves in the sun or hung unexpectedly on a stray gust of wind – Jason caught them all. Ground balls he picked up with perfect ease. It was wonderful. It was magnificent. It even made his batting average (which was very close to zero) seem less awful. His arm was a bit sore, of course. The glove tended to yank him around the outfield. It seemed to cry always too slow, too slow, hurry, hurry, hurry. Then, just when Jason was going full out, the glove grabbed him up sharply and seemed to cry wait, wait, wait. At the last possible minute it would almost trip him up by taking him one carefully calculated step to the right. Oh, but it was worth it. It was worth it!

'You did great, Jason,' said Penny after the game. They were walking with Spider and Oakly to pick up their bikes beside the stands.

'He finally learned to catch the ball,' said Oakly. 'Big deal. Did you see that homer I hit?'

'Oakly, you're so full of yourself, one day you'll just explode. Boom!' replied Penny. 'What I think is that if we all keep playing like this our team is going to be able to beat Westmoor Ridge this year. Nobody from around here has ever beaten the Ridge kids that I can remember. That would be really something. What do you think, Spider?'

Spider shrugged. 'It's pretty hard to do when we're not going to have a ball park to practise in, let alone play in.'

The four of them looked west down Poplar Street. Far at the end, perhaps a mile from the park but coming visibly closer every day, was the work crew with their bulldozers and loaders and dump trucks. Poplar Street was being widened to let the growing stream of traffic move more freely in its rush downtown and back again. The ball park was going under pavement. The open strip of grass beyond the diamond, the long line of poplar trees that bordered the road, and the little wild area of trees and bushes that skirted around the end were going under as well. If it had been a wide, broad park, some of it could have been saved. But it wasn't. The park was long and narrow. 'A pretty scrap of land', was how the local paper had put it when the road widening project had been announced.

'Stupid, stupid, stupid road!' said Oakly. He

picked up a rock and chucked it hard at a pop can on top of the stands. 'Why do they have to rip up our park? Why not just bulldoze the old houses on the other side of the road. They're all ugly old houses. They should just run them all down. That way we'd get rid of old man Becker too.'

Silas Becker lived beside the corner grocery store on Poplar Street. He was not fond of children. Children were not at all fond of him.

'Great,' said Penny. 'Except that Spider happens to live in one of those houses.'

'So?' said Oakly.

'So,' said Penny.

'So, he can move,' said Oakly. 'You can move, can't you, Spider?'

Spider chose not to answer. Instead, he lifted his bike from beside the stands and swung lazily aboard. His long, tall body rode loose and perfectly upright away from them. Spider seldom bothered to hold on to the handlebars.

'Oakly, you jerk,' said Penny. 'Did you ever see where Spider used to live? It's not a place anyone would want to move back to.'

'Big deal. He can move someplace else. Right, Jason?' said Oakly.

It was probably the first time Oakly Barnes had asked for Jason's opinion on anything, but Jason hadn't been paying attention. He had been looking at the cottonwood tree, way down at the end of the park. Was he there? Was that him sitting half way up or was it just the leaves turning and catching the sunlight? Maybe it was all a dream – the glove, the magical Quicksilver, the great and wondrous wishes that Jason had ready to wish. Jason couldn't wait any longer to find out.

'I've got to go,' said Jason.

He jumped on his bike and began to pedal across the grass.

'Jason,' called Penny. 'Jason, aren't you coming for a pop?'

'See you later,' Jason called back over his shoulder. Then he just kept pedalling, as hard and as fast as he could across the soft park grass.

3

Quicksilver was sitting cross-legged on the ground in a small clearing. The clearing was like a little room, or a leafy cave really, for it was bordered tightly by bushes and shaded from above by the cottonwood tree. Around him were three great piles of very thick books. Half the books were bound in red and half were bound in yellow. In his lap was a thin book bound in purple. Jason recognized his own name written backwards on the cover.

'I've been reading about you,' said Quicksilver, glancing up as Jason crawled in beneath the bushes. 'Frankly, I wish I had done it sooner.'

He closed the book and took off the pair of wire-rimmed glasses he had been wearing. He watched thoughtfully as Jason settled himself on the ground.

'How does the glove work?' he asked.

'Great! Oh just great!' replied Jason. 'I caught five fly balls and I forget how many grounders.'

'It's a success then?' asked Quicksilver.

'Oh yes, thank you,' replied Jason.

'Would you like to wish for a bat to go with it?' asked Quicksilver. 'I can do a magic bat that can hit any ball any time any place.'

Jason's eyes lit up. He wanted very much to wish for just such a bat.

'No,' said Jason regretfully.

'Would you like to wish for a brand new bike then?' asked Quicksilver. 'A ten-speed perhaps?'

Jason couldn't help glancing over his shoulder to where his battered old three-speed bike rested behind the bushes.

'No,' he said.

'How about a one year's supply of tickets to the movies?' pressed Quicksilver. 'A homework machine – especially for maths? Your very own dog?'

He was obviously aware of all of Jason's weaknesses. It was making things very hard for Jason.

'No,' said Jason.

'Well,' said Quicksilver impatiently. 'What *do* you wish for?'

'I was hoping,' began Jason. 'I was hoping . . . that is if you don't mind . . . if it's not too much trouble . . .'

'Out with it. Out with it!' said Quicksilver.

Jason took a deep breath.

'I wish that everybody in the whole world was rich. I don't mean super rich. I just mean rich enough to have enough food and clothes and a chance to go to see a ball game once a week or whatever they do where they live.

'That's wish number one but don't do anything yet because wish number two goes along with it.'

'I see,' said Quicksilver sternly. 'And what is wish number two?'

'No more fighting,' said Jason. He said it in a very sensible, very practical voice. 'Wish number two is no more fighting, especially wars, but also the small mean type. I wish that.'

'And?' asked Quicksilver.

'And what?' asked Jason.

'Wish number three?' asked Quicksilver.

'Well, I'd like to see how the first two work before I try the third one,' explained Jason.

Quicksilver nodded. He looked very stern. He

sat looking stern for quite a long time. The longer he sat the sterner he looked.

Jason was about to speak when Quicksilver lowered his head and set both hands to his temples. Suddenly Jason heard it. It was the sound again. It echoed all around him and raced through him the way the wind races hollowly through a long, long pipe lying at the side of a deserted road. The sound went on for a long time. When it stopped, Quicksilver looked sterner than ever. He looked so stern that Jason was quite afraid to talk to him.

Jason crept to the edge of the bushes. He looked out at the neighbourhood he knew so well. That park was still there, the busy street, the row of older houses across the way where Spider and old Silas Becker lived. The taller buildings of downtown were still there, way beyond the houses. In the other direction, up Top Hill, the old Central Library building still sat looking out over the city. And yet, was Jason imagining it, or did everything feel splendidly fresh and new?

Suddenly, Jason heard a shriek of outrage. He turned his head just in time to see Mel Flynn finish kicking the spokes out of some smaller kid's bike and run off hooting with laughter. The same thing had happened to Jason two weeks before. Jason pulled his head back in among the bushes. He looked at Quicksilver.

'I don't think it worked,' said Jason.

'I didn't think it would,' said Quicksilver unhappily.

'Too big?' asked Jason.

'Not exactly,' he said. 'It simply – as you said – didn't work. The kind that generally don't work are the kind that interfere in other people's lives too much. That, most certainly, is what did us in.'

'But a wish is a wish and a deal is a deal,' protested Jason.

'Arguing won't change things,' interrupted Quicksilver. 'I can grant wishes for *you* – Jason Arthur Reid. The rest of the world is going to have to do things the hard way.'

'Then all you can really grant is greedy little self-centred wishes,' said Jason with considerable disappointment.

'That's all you're expected to wish for in the first place!' said Quicksilver crossly. 'Look. Haven't you been paying attention to all the stories about us? You're supposed to wish for greedy, selfish things and then you're expected to mess up because you're so greedy and selfish and in the end you're supposed to have learned a lesson and that's that.'

'I don't like it,' said Jason.

'I thought you might not,' said Quicksilver wearily. 'That's why I brought the books.' He gestured to the great piles of thick books around him. 'The Complete Laws of Wishes. You may have found one loophole but you won't find another. There are no others. Read about it for yourself.'

Jason looked at the tall pile of books and then he looked at Quicksilver and then he looked back at the books again.

'You know, I really did try,' said Quicksilver. 'That's more than most would do. I wanted to at least try because those are the wishes I'd have liked best to pull off, if I could.'

'Really?' asked Jason.

'Really,' Quicksilver replied. He cleared his throat and brushed a leaf off the lapel of his coat. 'And besides, you've still got one last wish. What will it be? How about the bike?'

'One last wish!' said Jason. 'But you couldn't do the first two so I should get them over again.'

'No, no,' said Quicksilver. 'It's all covered in here.' He gestured to the large stacks of red and yellow books. 'As I said, I thought we might have a bit of trouble, so I brought them, just in case.'

He snapped his fingers and a book removed itself from one of the piles and appeared open in Jason's hands. Jason squinted at the peculiar curls and lines.

'Sorry,' said Quicksilver. With a wave of his hand he turned the page into words that Jason could read. It was rather complicated and Jason was working hard to read the whole chapter, but in the end Quicksilver was right.

'It's not fair,' said Jason.

'None the less, it's in the book,' said Quicksilver. 'Now, quick, your third wish. You can't take all day. Quick. Quick. Quick.'

Jason pulled his hat down low over his eyes.

'I wish for three more wishes,' he said.

'You rotten little stinker!' said Quicksilver.

The pile of red books disappeared with a poof.

Quicksilver turned three times and disappeared with a poof. Jason climbed out of the bushes, jumped on his bicycle and rode home.

4

Three wishes. Three wishes. Three greedy, self-centred wishes. Jason had not realized before how hard it would be to decide. There were so many nice, greedy, self-centred wishes to choose from.

A new bike, a trip to the moon and . . . thought Jason.

A swimming pool in the back yard, an interview with a real dragon and . . . thought Jason.

He always made his choices that way in his mind: one object, one adventure, and for the third wish . . . well, why not wish for more wishes? Why not keep on wishing and wishing forever?

Jason sat on the front steps of his house. His mind was working a million miles a minute and he was getting absolutely nowhere. Something was wrong. It was getting too hard. It was too hard keeping it all to himself. He had to talk to somebody.

Penny, thought Jason. She would understand. He had to find Penny.

Jason jumped on his bike and rode to her house. She wasn't there. He found her at the park, hanging upside down on the monkey bars. Her long brown hair hung down below her like a gravity-bound halo. It isn't easy talking to someone hanging upside down and weird-looking but Jason's words just came pouring out. He told her about Quicksilver and the wishes and the books and the mitt and the magic. All at once and very fast he told her. Penny did a somersault and landed with a thunk in the gravel.

'You're nuts,' said Penny.

'No, I'm not!' said Jason. 'Look. My mitt, see? It's magic. That's why I caught all those fly balls at the game yesterday. I can catch any ball any place any time. I just tell the mitt I want to catch it and I do. Look.'

Jason threw the ball high in the air and closed his eyes tight.

'Mitt, catch the ball,' he cried.

The glove took him five steps to the right, pulled his arm up and caught the ball.

'See,' said Jason excitedly. 'It's magic!'

'What mitt?' asked Penny.

'This mitt,' cried Jason loudly. 'This mitt right here!'

'Perfectly normal mitt,' said Penny calmly. Then Jason remembered, for, of course, those had been his exact words. Penny could never recognize his magic mitt. He had wished that nobody would be able to recognize it.

Jason slumped on to the grass dejectedly. It wasn't fair.

'I wish you could understand,' he said unhappily. 'I wish you knew all about it. I wish . . .'

'Stop!' cried Penny.

Jason clapped his hand over his mouth. He looked at Penny. Her eyes were wide and dark. His wishes had come true. She understood. She knew all about Quicksilver and the books and the sound like the wind through a culvert. He had been right. The wishes did happen any time, any place. They had been happening right now.

'Quick,' said Penny. 'Do something. You've left your last wish just hanging there.'

'I wish for three more wishes,' said Jason loudly.

A muttering, buzzing noise brooded in the air around them. Then with a loud snap the air was still. Penny looked around them cautiously.

'It's all right now,' said Jason. 'I think he's gone. I almost blew it that time, though, I'm glad . . .'

'Wait, wait,' said Penny. She pressed the palms of her hands against her forehead.

'What's wrong?' asked Jason.

'I don't know,' said Penny. 'I guess it's just all those things you wished into my mind. My mind feels crammed to the point of bursting. Just let it work a while. O K?'

Jason nodded. Penny lay back on the grass. She was thinking very hard. Jason did his best not to speak. It was very hard not to. It is very hard not to blabber unendingly when you have had something very unusual inside of you for four days.

Jason rolled on to his stomach and looked far down the length of the park. Way at the end a man was walking slowly among the large poplar trees that lined the road. Old Silas Becker was on patrol. He chased out anyone he found climbing in those trees. He knocked apart any makeshift treehouse he found with a stout cane he carried especially for that purpose. Jason wondered what Silas Becker would do if he knocked at something in one of his trees and Quicksilver came tumbling out. Oh well. Quicksilver could take care of himself.

'OK,' said Penny at last. 'I think I've got it straight.' She sat up on the grass. Jason could see by her eyes that she was still thinking about things pretty hard.

'How much do you know?' he asked.

'I think I know everything,' replied Penny. 'That's what you wished, wasn't it?'

'Do you know about . . .' Jason swallowed once, he felt rather silly . . . 'about all my wishes?'

'Sure,' said Penny. 'I know about all of them. And you needn't act so odd about it. You're not the only one alive who'd rather do something on a grand scale than have a new bicycle.'

'Oh,' said Jason. He was rather relieved, but just a little let down too.

'Actually, I would have done it a bit different,' said Penny. 'I would have wished myself to be the sole ruling monarch of the whole world and then . . .'

'It wouldn't have worked,' said Jason shaking his head. 'I've thought it all out before, you see. If you put yourself in charge, then you've got lots of power but you don't know what to do with it to make things go the way you want them to. You've got to wish the changes themselves. It's the only real hope.'

'Well, maybe,' said Penny. 'Anyway, it doesn't matter. Things on the grand scale seem to be against the rules, whatever they are. Still, there must be some way we can wish something really worthwhile. That's why you brought me in on this, isn't it?'

Jason looked at Penny. Now that he had done it, he didn't really know why, except that he couldn't keep things to himself any longer. As to doing something special – he'd almost given that up.

Or had he? Looking at Penny sitting cross-legged and already deep in thought on the grass, Jason realized she was right. If he had wanted to amass scads of goodies he would have thrown in with Oakly. If he had wanted fame and fortune he would have thrown in with Spider and they would have both been off to the Expos' training camp. But he had thrown in with Penny.

There were going to be some special wishes after all.

5

'Here's something!'

Jason lifted the book that lay open in his lap and handed it across to Penny. They were sitting on the floor of Jason's bedroom. Around them lay books of all shape and description. Among the books were scattered lists of ideas ranging from a telescope that would 'see' the far reaches of the galaxy to a mechanical policing system for the streets after midnight. On the floor between Jason and Penny was a large, hand-drawn chart on which they were trying to organize their thoughts.

Penny took the book and began to read.

'It says there that before they became extinct there were so many of them that they used to blacken the sky when they flew,' said Jason, not waiting for her to finish reading. 'And now there isn't even one. Anywhere.'

Penny looked up at him.

'We could bring them back,' said Jason matter-of-factly. 'Jason Arthur Reid and Penny Angela Mitten could bring back the passenger pigeon!'

'We could?' said Penny.

'We could,' said Jason.

'We could,' said Penny, 'if we knew for certain they'd still fit in. If we knew for certain that their nesting grounds weren't needed by other birds, we could, and if we knew there were still places for them to feed and we weren't going to wipe out something else by bringing them back.'

Jason frowned.

'The problem is,' said Penny, 'everything we come up with either interferes too much or it's so far fetched that even I can't see it working. This job isn't going to be as easy as I thought.'

'I know,' said Jason.

'I'll write down passenger pigeon in the "just maybe possible" column anyway,' said Penny. 'What about Quicksilver? Have you seen him lately?'

'No,' said Jason. He was a bit uneasy about that question himself. It had been four days now since he had actually seen Quicksilver. The wishes, however, kept working just fine. In fact, they worked in batches much closer together than

Jason had at first hoped for. They worked in batches much closer together than even Penny knew.

Penny began to write on the chart again. Jason leafed through another book. He wasn't really paying attention. He was thinking. He wanted to tell Penny about what had been happening lately with the wishes but he was afraid to. Quite truthfully, he wasn't sure whether it was a side effect of the magic or his own private greed. All he knew was that by remembering they had bigger things in mind he had at least managed to keep some kind of control on it. For now, that would have to be good enough.

Jason looked at the books and papers strewn around the room. A sense of hopelessness set in. There were so many ideas and none of them were right. It was all getting far too complicated for Jason. Jason liked things clear and clean and sharp.

'What if we just took one war in one place and did one little thing that would help end the whole mess?' he said.

Penny smiled but shook her head.

'We don't have the kind of inside information you need to do something like that,' she said.

'I guess you're right,' Jason regretfully admitted.

'Look Jason, don't worry. We'll find something,' said Penny. She finished writing and sat back again on the rug. 'What time is it?'

'Just after eight,' said Jason.

'I've got to get home,' said Penny, 'but I'll keep thinking about it. You're coming to baseball practice tomorrow after school, aren't you?'

'I'm coming, all right,' said Jason. He glanced to where his mitt lay in hallowed honour on the pillow of his bed.

'Good,' said Penny. 'Spider doesn't think there'll be any trouble beating the Riverside kids when they come Saturday, but we've got to get in all the practice we can.'

When Penny had gone Jason lay a long while on his bed. He wasn't thinking exactly. He was just letting things pass over him. Finally he got up and slipped on his jacket. He tucked his baseball glove inside, close against his shirt. Then he went outside.

It was dusk. The little shed behind Jason's house sat as calmly and quietly as ever. No one used the shed since his dad had built the garage. Just in case, however, Jason had wished the door stuck shut to anyone but himself. He slipped quickly inside. He double checked that the window was blocked off and turned on the light.

Inside the shed there were a new ten-speed bike that changed gears just by the rider thinking about it; a dinosaur book with real, living pictures; a scrabble game that would, itself, be the competitor when nobody else wanted to play; a large red kite that flew with the mind's eye; an exquisitely strung guitar that Jason had not yet dared to play.

Jason looked at each item for a moment. Then he stood back a little.

'I wish for a skate board that can go up hills as well as down. I wish for an aquarium, full of fish, that never needs its water changed. I wish for three more wishes,' he said.

The skate board appeared hanging on the wall beside him. Jason ran his hand along the smoothness of its body and rolled the wonderfully free and carefully balanced wheels.

He looked around for the fish tank. It was on a shelf at the back of the shed. Jason walked over

and peered into it. It was as big as the largest
tank he had ever seen in any of the stores and it
was filled, not with the goldfish and common
angel fish that he had expected, but with marine
fish. There were copperband butterfly fish,
powder-blue surgeon-fish, neon goby and ex-
quisite sea horses that curled and uncurled their
tails and fanned the water with fins like wings in
the most delicate motions. Jason stared and stared
and stared.

'What did you expect? Guppies?'

Jason spun around. Quicksilver was sitting on the handlebars of the ten-speed. He looked not quite the same as Jason had remembered him, not quite as solid somehow. However the light was poor and unflattering and certainly his voice was as crisply sharp as ever.

'They're beautiful,' said Jason.

'Thank you,' said Quicksilver. 'But what I really want to know is whether or not you're ever going to tire of this. Every night for four nights now you've been at it. It would be a lot easier on both of us if you'd just wish for something large and let us be over and done with.'

'I'm afraid if I do it that way I'll make a mistake,' said Jason. 'I don't want to make a mistake.'

'No,' said Quicksilver, in a dark tone of voice, 'I can see that. You've even taken an accomplice to see how much you can get out of me.'

'It's not like that at all,' explained Jason quickly. 'Honestly. Penny is helping me think of something special to wish for — not something on such a grand scale that you can't make it work, but something that would be really worthwhile anyway.'

Quicksilver lifted one eyebrow.

'And all this?' he asked.

'It's just here,' said Jason stubbornly. 'It's not like I've used any of it.'

Quicksilver looked at Jason and Jason looked at Quicksilver and it was Jason who looked away first. He climbed up on one of the old work benches and sat across from Quicksilver with his legs hanging over the edge.

'I don't seem to be able to stop myself,' said Jason matter-of-factly. 'I started wishing just for little things – like getting to school on time the day I woke up late – and somehow it just kept on going. I don't know what would have happened if I hadn't thought of keeping everything locked up in the shed. So long as it's all in here it's like . . . well it's like I'm still in charge. But it isn't easy. The part I really don't understand is that once I've wished for something I don't even really want it any more.' He looked around him but stopped when he reached the aquarium. 'Except the fish. The fish really are wonderful.'

Quicksilver nodded and straightened his coat.

'I think it's time we called it quits,' he said.

'No,' said Jason. And then he said it a little bit louder. 'No. Not yet. I've thought about it and thought about it. One ought to be able to do one special thing with wishes or what's the use? And that's what I'm going to do.'

Quicksilver looked at Jason a long time. Then, with an expression on his face that Jason could not quite understand, he shook his head.

'Trust it to happen when it's my turn to step through,' he said.

'Step through?' asked Jason, looking across at him.

'Never mind,' said Quicksilver. 'It may work out yet. It always has before.'

'But step through what? You keep talking about stepping through. Step through *time*?' asked Jason. He had a rather unsettling thought. 'Step through me?'

'No, no,' said Quicksilver with a frown. 'It's nothing as complicated as that. You don't have to be worried about it. It's just a very old term. It means simply stepping through the human world. In one side and out the other, so to speak. Except for this three wishes business in between.'

Jason's eyes grew very wide.

'What do you mean "the human world"? Are there other worlds? Outer space worlds?'

'I've no idea what's in outer space,' said Quicksilver quietly.

Jason reached up to pull down his baseball cap, but it wasn't there. He was going to have to think bareheaded and somehow that wasn't quite as easy.

'But in order to get through here, my world, you have to grant three wishes to someone,' he said slowly.

'Yes,' said Quicksilver.

'And it's happened before,' said Jason. 'The old fairy tales with the three wishes . . . you, or someone like you.'

'Perhaps,' Quicksilver replied with a private smile.

Jason opened his mouth to speak again but Quicksilver raised his hands.

'It's an ancient, ancient pact between your ancestors and mine and there isn't much more that you could understand, even if I told you.' As he spoke, Quicksilver began to fade slowly, becoming delicately transparent. 'Turn out the light before you leave. I don't want you waking me up in the middle of the night so you can wish to have it turned off. I'm not quite feeling up to par lately.'

'Wait. Please!' Jason called after him. 'Just one more question.'

'Only one,' said Quicksilver.

Jason knew he had to hurry. Quicksilver was almost gone now. He was just a shadow against the dark wood of the shed.

'What does it feel like when you step through?' asked Jason. 'When you go from your world into ours or from ours into wherever you're going, what does it feel like?'

The answer came in the form of a question, clear and unhurried, from the very air itself.

'Have you ever pushed through a perfectly balanced revolving door?'

6

Jason and Penny did not come up with the special wishes Thursday after practice. They did not think of the perfect solution Friday after school. When Saturday morning rolled around the main thing on their minds was baseball.

It was Saturday morning, in fact, when Jason decided that just being able to catch the ball wasn't good enough any more.

He was standing out in the rough grass of left field watching Spider pitch the first innings against the Riverside team when the decision planted itself in his mind. Spider pitched smooth. Spider pitched with class. When Spider caught the ball, every muscle in his body knew perfectly what it was doing. Then and there Jason decided. If he was going to field the ball from now on, he too was going to do it with style.

It was, after all, only a matter of practice. With the mitt to do the actual catching for him Jason could try everything and anything until he found the way that felt just right.

Jason mapped out his area in the outfield. The centre fielder was down with the measles and right fielder liked to play far right so Jason took over all the territory in between.

He tried catching the ball with his arms high over his head. He tried catching with his elbows close against his sides. He tried every position in between. He watched with fascination the way the ball arched through the air – he had all the time in the world to watch the ball now that he didn't have to worry about catching it. He over-ran the ball on purpose and then, with the glove to assure his success, he stepped coolly forward to make the catch. He learned how to cushion the impact of a hard, straight drive in the muscles of his arms and shoulders. He learned to swoop down upon grounders with professional ease. The better he got at it the more it fascinated him. It was a magical combination – the ball, the mitt, and Jason the invincible outfielder.

His own part in the game went so well that it was rather hard for Jason to believe, as the bottom of the ninth innings began, that they were losing the game.

Riverside was a most peculiar team. The pitcher was short and fat with stubby, round, red hands that made Jason think of tomatoes. The back catcher had a scar on his cheek and wore a black cowboy hat. The short stop was tall and skinny with yellow tinted glasses that looked like they were at least two inches thick. The third baseman didn't own a glove. Oakly had sneered when he had first seen them. But he hadn't sneered for long.

The Riverside team couldn't hit or field particularly well but they did have one single, carefully developed talent. They stole bases. Not just one or two of the players stole bases. All of them did. Every member was fast. Every member was sneaky. Every member, even the pitcher, could slide as low and flat and cunningly as a snake.

Their game plan had been simple. One player got on at first. He stole his way to second. He stole his way to third. Finally, with an enormous surge of will power, the Riverside team would put everything they had into getting that one man home. One man an innings crossed home plate. After that the team collapsed as if the effort had been too great, but they always got that one man home. When the bottom of the ninth began, Riverside had nine neat runs against the seven Jason's team had marked up.

'This is ridiculous,' said Oakly, who was first up. 'They've only hit two single base hits an innings and they've been scoring runs. They don't even know how to play decent baseball and they're beating us!' He went up to bat and slammed a homer so hard that the ball sailed clear into Silas Becker's trees and bounced off one with a terrible whack.

'I've done my bit,' said Oakly, trotting in from third. He sat down on the bench and glared pointedly at the players next up to bat.

'That's what I like about Oakly Barnes,' said Penny as she went up to bat. 'He just overflows with team spirit and good sportsmanship.'

Jason heard her but did not reply. He was part of the game and he knew what was happening, but his infatuation with his glove had led him to think of other things. He was thinking about the way people moved when they played baseball.

He was thinking about the way people caught the ball, the way they swung their bat. He was thinking about how the ball cut its way through the air. It was only through all his thinking that he saw Penny single and Greg strike out. And then Speedball Willie, the short stop, doubled his way on to second base and Penny to third. One run down. Two men on. Bottom of the ninth.

'You're up next, Jason,' said Spider.

Jason jumped in spite of himself. He didn't need to be told he was next, of course. It was a sign that Spider was very, very worried about the outcome of the game. As he went up to the plate Jason was thankful that there was only one down so far. At least when he struck out, the entire game wouldn't fall on his shoulders. And he would strike out. At a practice, maybe, he could hit the ball. Early on in a game when no one was really watching anyway, he might hit the ball. He had never, however, ever hit any kind of ball in the ninth.

Jason stood at the plate with his hands sweated tightly together on the neck of the bat. Doomed though it was to failure, he always made the effort. Hit the ball. Hit the ball. He repeated the words over and over in his mind. It was what he always said to himself when he came to bat. As the pitcher wound up, Jason's eyes fell on his fat red hands and Jason's mind slipped into a different line of thought.

The way the ball flew high and hard when hit off a bat was one thing. The way it came spinning out of a pitcher's hand had to be considerably different. It was something that had never occurred to him before and it caught his newly whetted interest.

And that was why Jason was watching, really watching, when the Riverside pitcher threw him the fast ball. It would probably never happen that way as long as he lived but this time Jason sensed where the ball was going as it flashed towards him. He swung his bat. Crack.

He had hit it! He had really hit it – not hard, not far, but hard enough and far enough for Penny to come burning in from third with Speedball Willie hot on her heels.

The bench exploded. Astonished cheers surrounded Jason as he trotted back from first base. Players slapped him on the shoulders. Oakly slapped him hard on the back. Spider turned his hat sideways on his head. Only Penny stood to one side, watching the ruckus with a guarded expression.

'Did you wish it?' asked Penny.

They were sitting on their bikes waiting for Spider and Oakly. Spider and Oakly were getting pointers on how to steal bases from the Riverside back catcher. It wasn't only Jason's team who wanted to see the kids from Westmoor Ridge beaten for a change.

'Wish what?' asked Jason. He'd just at that moment been thinking about feeding the fish when he got home. He looked at Penny suspiciously.

'My run. Willie's run. Your hit. Did you do it with a wish?'

'Oh that,' said Jason with a smile. 'No. I didn't wish that. I got lucky.'

'Good,' said Penny, relief showing clearly across her face.

'What do you mean?' asked Jason.

'Just good,' said Penny. 'And are you going to let him go afterwards? Quicksilver? Are you going to let him go after the special wishes?'

'We haven't got the special wishes yet,' said Jason.

'I know, but we'll find something soon. Are you going to let him go?' she pressed.

Jason nodded.

'I don't think he could last forever even if I wanted him to,' said Jason. 'But I don't see why you have to make it sound as if I'd captured him or something. He started it.'

'I know. I know. It's just that . . .' Penny paused. 'Jason, I'm not entirely certain but I think that what I know about Quicksilver is a little different from what you know about him. What I know got put into my mind and it wasn't just the facts. There was a feeling about things too. I know he started it. But I'm glad that you're going to let him go.'

7

Silas Becker stood on his back steps and looked out at the world. He was big and he was baggy. He had thick eyebrows that went shooting off in every direction like an oddly flattened bottle brush. He watched Oakly, Penny, Jason and Spider lean their bikes against the corner store and go inside. They knew better than to lean their bikes against Silas Becker's fence, especially when Silas was watching them.

It was a Wednesday night strategy session, called late by Spider. Jason, for one, had been glad to attend. He and Penny still hadn't come up with the perfect special wishes. Jason wasn't sure that they would ever come up with them. More and more he felt as if he was being pulled in two directions and yet he couldn't give up on either of them – neither the special wishes nor the hoard of goodies that grew nightly in the shed.

The four friends bought cheesies and pop and

went out back of the store where their bikes were parked. There was a heavy old pop cooler they could sit on, and there was less noise from the traffic that rolled in endless waves down Poplar Street.

'Westmoor Ridge is coming down on Saturday,' said Spider, snapping open the lid of his pop can.

'What?' asked Penny. 'I thought we were going to practise and make sure we could beat them before they came down?'

'No time,' said Spider. 'I talked to one of the men on the construction crew yesterday. They're coming through the park next week. If we're going to play the Ridge at all we may as well play them on our home ground.'

'We'll take them,' said Oakly. 'They're all a bunch of jerks.'

'We could use a lot more practice,' said Penny.

'We'll take them anyways, won't we, Spider?' said Oakly with assurance.

Spider lifted his shoulders in a loose shrug and smiled his half smile. Oakly didn't notice. Glancing around them he had found something else he liked to talk about.

'Look at old man Becker,' said Oakly. 'He just stands there and stares like an old goon. You can't hardly sit around the store any more, let alone touch a tree in the park, without old man Becker getting after you. After he goes inside let's dump his rubbish across his lawn.'

Spider looked sideways at Oakly. Penny and Jason looked the other way.

'You bunch of chickens,' said Oakly.

It was the wrong thing to say. No one called Spider a chicken. Spider glowered thoughtfully at Oakly for a bit. Then he slid off the pop cooler and sauntered over to Silas Becker's fence. He leaned full against the fence, swigging on his pop with cool nonchalance.

'Big trouble,' said Oakly in a small voice.

Jason drew his breath in through his teeth. Penny frowned hard across at Spider.

Silas Becker came down the steps from his house. Jason saw that he carried a long, narrow garden shovel in his left hand as he crossed the yard. He moved slowly, with a burly sense of purpose. He stopped across the fence just beside Spider. Spider turned his head and looked up at him. Silas Becker stood looking down at

Spider from beneath his wild and wiry eye-brows.

'You're the pitcher,' he said.

Spider tilted his head ten degrees forward and then returned it to centre.

'Your fast ball needs work,' said Becker.

Spider's eyebrows drew sharply together.

'But your curve makes up for it.'

Spider's lip lifted one centimetre on the right side.

They both turned and stood looking towards where Oakly and Penny and Jason were perched on the pop cooler behind the store. Jason couldn't help but notice how Spider instinctively took on the old man's expression, looking out upon a world that was both puzzling and hostile. Jason much preferred the cool, youthful Spider.

'Where are you going to practise your fast ball when they run the road through the park?' asked Becker abruptly.

'I've played in back alleys before,' said Spider.

Silas Becker nodded.

'Tough kid, eh,' he said. Then he shrugged. 'Why not? They take everything anyway. They're taking the ball park. And the trees. Do you know how old those trees are? My grandfather planted those trees. They're over a hundred years old.'

Spider looked up at the man.

'The bunch of fools at City Hall! They wanted to take these houses too,' said Becker. 'I for one told them that if they wanted me out they'd have to tunnel underneath and plant dynamite and blow me out. I'm still giving them plenty of trouble over the park, but there isn't any way now that we're going to save it.'

Spider's eyes squinted up into Becker's own. Jason sensed that for once Spider would have liked to say something but he couldn't quite find the right words.

'Don't lean on the fence, son,' said Becker and went over around the house to dig his garden. He didn't bother looking back.

'What a creep,' said Oakly as they climbed on their bikes. He lifted his shoulders and lowered his eyebrows and deepened his voice in imitation. '"My grandfather planted those trees. Get off the fence, son." Who'd want to be related to an old crock like that.'

Spider walked up to Oakly real close and looked into his face.

'I'm getting really tired of you lately, Oakly,' he said. 'Do you know what I mean?'

Oakly gulped once and turned slightly soft.

'All right. All right,' he said. 'But I'm entitled to think what I like and I still think he's an old crock.' Oakly spun a wheelie out on to the street and raced off on his bike.

Penny looked at Spider.

'The only thing Oakly likes better than climbing trees is playing baseball,' she said. Spider nodded. Then he swung on to his bike.

'Tell the other kids,' he said. 'Practice tomorrow night. We play the Ridge on Saturday. And that's it for the ball park.' He headed on down the alley home.

Penny and Jason looked after Spider. Then they looked at Becker's old house. Then they looked at the gravel where Oakly had spun out. Then they looked at each other.

Of one mind, Penny and Jason rode their bikes over to the park. They rode down the grass to the far end where the trees grew a little bit wild and the cottonwood lorded over all. They stood in the shadow of its leaves and looked at the little scrap of greenery penned hard against the traffic.

'We could do it,' said Penny. 'It's perfect. It's been here under our noses all along but I just couldn't see it!'

She looked hopefully at Jason. 'It would be for you and me too, of course. That wouldn't spoil things, would it?'

'It wouldn't be just for us,' said Jason. 'It would be for Spider and Oakly and the rest of the kids and Silas Becker and maybe for lots of other people who use this park or just like to know it's here!' Jason could barely hold the excitement within him. 'But how, Penny? If we start sending the cars way out and around we're sure to run into trouble. And we can't just block it off. How can we do it?'

'I know a way,' said Penny, nodding to herself. She broke into a grin that grew wider and wider. 'It's the only way and it's perfect. Come on, Jason! We have work to do!'

8

'You want me to do *what*?' asked Quicksilver in disbelief.

'We want you to build a tunnel,' said Jason.

Quicksilver sat cross-legged in the little space beneath the cottonwood tree and frowned at Penny and Jason. Jason looked evenly back. Penny, who had never seen him before, watched Quicksilver with interested eyes. Across her knees she held a large, carefully rolled up piece of paper.

'No,' said Quicksilver.

'What do you mean, no?' asked Jason, a little upset.

Quicksilver looked pointedly at the large roll of paper.

'No,' he repeated.

'It's just a tunnel,' said Jason. 'But it's rather an important tunnel so we wanted to do it right.'

'The way you did your glove right?' asked Quicksilver.

'Something like that,' said Jason.

'I see,' said Quicksilver and he scowled even harder.

'What's wrong?' asked Jason.

Quicksilver sat silently for a few moments.

'It's a most uncomfortable feeling really,' he said at last. He looked down at his feet and then back at Jason. 'Frankly, this whole business is taking a good deal more out of me than it should. And now, you two come up with a tunnel.'

Jason pulled his hat down low over his eyes and looked out from beneath it. He wasn't sure exactly what was going on here. Quicksilver did look a little thinner and a little ragged around the edges but at the same time there was, and had always been, a slight air of the theatrical about his person.

Jason looked at Quicksilver and Quicksilver looked at Jason. The longer they looked at each other, the more apparent it became that each was determinedly waiting for the other to make the next move. The little leafy cave became very, very quiet.

'Maybe,' said Penny in a small voice, 'maybe

you could just, at least, perhaps, look at what we've got?'

Quicksilver lifted his head and looked at her sharply. Before he could reply Penny spread out the plans she and Jason had worked on the last few days. The three of them bent over the paper intently. Penny pointed out some of the main ideas that they had tried to include in the drawing. Quicksilver peered and peered and finally sat back with a frown.

'You expect me, in my state, to move umpteen tons of sand, rock and gravel, shore it up, smooth it, pave it, beautify it, ventilate it, light it!'

Jason felt the disappointment like a hard knot inside him.

'If you can't do it, just say so,' he said quietly.

Quicksilver looked from Jason to Penny and back again.

'Well,' he said. And then again, 'Well.' He seemed to be weighing something very carefully in his mind. He straightened his coat and rubbed a crease in the toe of his soft shoes. Jason and Penny did not speak. 'Well,' said Quicksilver again. 'How many wishes would you be using for this tunnel of yours?'

Taking his cue from Quicksilver, Jason pushed aside his disappointment and pulled on his negotiating hat.

'Three,' said Jason.

'Three?' asked Quicksilver. 'No rewish?'

'No rewish,' replied Jason.

'Absolutely no rewish?' asked Quicksilver.

'Absolutely no rewish,' answered Jason.

'Tell me more,' said Quicksilver.

Penny took a sheet of paper out of her back pocket. She unfolded it carefully and read from it.

'Wish number one. Eight lane tunnel to be built under Poplar Street and adjoining park from Knox Street to Fourth Street.'

'Six,' said Quicksilver firmly.

Jason thought quickly. In truth, the extra lanes had been only a safeguard against further expansion.

'Six,' he agreed. 'Three each way.' He nodded to Penny to go on.

'Number two. Tunnel to be perfectly sound and able to endure any type of disaster. Nobody to be hurt or displaced, or to experience loss of wages because of it.'

'You want a bomb shelter,' said Quicksilver.

'Not exactly,' said Jason. 'Just something soundly built.'

'And what is this loss of wages?' asked Quicksilver.

'That means the construction workers working on the road,' said Jason. 'We thought you could fix it, so they'd still be employed for the full summer.'

'I see,' said Quicksilver curtly and turned again to Penny.

'Number three. No one to question the tunnel's existence or to have it blocked off. Everyone to accept it. Everyone to think it is a perfectly normal tunnel.'

'I've heard that line before,' said Quicksilver.

'It worked well the first time,' said Jason.

'And that's that?' asked Quicksilver.

Jason nodded.

'Do you want to read it for yourself?' asked Penny. Quicksilver shook his head. Penny folded the paper carefully and tucked it back into her pocket. She rolled up the plans for the tunnel and held them across her knees. She looked at Jason and Jason shook his head.

'Are those really your wishes, your final three wishes?' asked Quicksilver.

'Those are my final three wishes,' said Jason.

Quicksilver put his chin in his hands and sat silently thinking. Above them Penny and Jason could hear a sighing sound as the evening air currents rose and fell among the leaves of the cottonwood.

'When?' asked Quicksilver finally.

Jason and Penny looked at each other, excitement welling between them.

'Tomorrow morning,' said Jason. 'Five a.m. First light.'

9

At five o'clock in the morning the city was only barely awake. Jason and Penny sat close together on the library steps on Top Hill. The air was fresh and new.

'We should have wished for the air to always be this clean,' said Jason.

'Jason, you're a dreamer,' said Penny. 'There's not many things in the world that can ever be fixed just by wishing, even if you have your own magical Elster of the Third Class, or whatever. I think we've done great just to get this one thing.'

'I'm really excited,' said Jason. 'I hope it works.'

'That is a bit of a concern,' said a voice behind them on the steps.

'Yikes!' said Jason. He turned to find Quicksilver standing there. 'I wish you wouldn't sneak up on people.'

'Too late,' smiled Quicksilver happily. 'All your wishes are used up.'

'Not yet,' said Jason. 'You haven't tried to do it yet.'

'I shall try immediately,' said Quicksilver. 'I just hope I'm up to it. Let's see those plans again.'

Penny held out the carefully drawn plans. Quicksilver took them from her and looked at them. He nodded and handed them back to Penny.

'I'm going to do the wishes out of order if you don't mind,' said Quicksilver. He sat beside them on the steps. 'I'll blanket in acceptance of the tunnel first and put a few delays into the work crew operation. Then, when the moment is just right, I'll lay the tunnel down sound and perfect under Poplar Street and the park. I'll do it slowly, so you can see it happen. It will be rather spectacular, actually, I've quite a flair for these things . . . when I'm up to it.'

Quicksilver turned his attention upon the view before him. Down the hill ran the older houses and narrow cross streets of the neighbourhood. Poplar Street, quiet now under the long fingers of early morning light, cut like a ribbon between them. It wove its way through the area that was under construction, ran straight and long beside the little green park and lost itself in the tall buildings that crowded in upon it from beyond.

Only a handful of cars moved along the street. There were no people to be seen but a dog padded south down the sidewalk. Across from the library a small wooden figure chopped wood as its windmill-powered workings turned squeakily in the early breeze.

Quicksilver shifted his shoulders. There was a moment of complete silence. Then the sound began, low and hollow. It was the sound of the wind through a pipe. It was faint at first and then grew, not exactly louder, but firmer, warmer.

'Everything's stopped!' gasped Jason. The cars, the dog, even the wind were suspended in time.

'Shhh,' said Penny.

Quicksilver was beginning to sway slightly. His face was quite pale. It was obvious that already he had begun to work under some strain.

'Look!' gasped Jason again, pointing down below them where Poplar met Knox Street. A patch of pavement the size of a manhole cover had begun to move. It was spinning and spinning. Then slowly, as if burrowing, it began to drop away, pulling an ever-widening cross-section of the road with it. Like a whirlwind spinning through a pile of sand it worked, except there was no wind. There just the spinning, spinning, deeper and deeper and down under Poplar Street. Behind it it left a wonderful tunnel that was wide and light and covered with some material that was white and coloured all at once like mother of pearl. And the tunnel was growing longer. Penny and Jason could see it as if through the eyes of Quicksilver himself. They could see it from above and they could see it making its way steadily beneath the earth as well. It was spinning, spinning, burrowing, growing, laying itself out under the park now. Right beneath the baseball diamond it travelled, beneath the outfield, beneath the trees where Jason had told Quicksilver his greatest wishes. Soon it would be past Sixth Street and then it would begin to rise again.

'What's wrong!' cried Jason suddenly. 'It's stopping!'

'Quicksilver,' cried Penny. 'Oh Jason. Look!'

He was sitting with his body rigidly rocking, rocking back and forth on the steps. He was shaking and rocking and his face was like an awful mask.

'Stop,' said Penny, urgently kneeling beside him. 'Stop. It's all right. You can stop.'

But it was obvious that Quicksilver could not or would not stop. He was caught in it. There was no letting go.

'How can we help him, Jason?' said Penny, turning desperately to him. 'Think. There must be something we can do!'

Jason was already thinking as hard as he could. He knew how determined Quicksilver could be. But what could he do? Quicksilver was the one with the magic. Jason had no special powers. He was just Jason. He had always been just Jason. No one could expect anything of him because he had nothing special to give. And yet there had to be something. When he found his voice it was heavy and hoarse.

'I give it all back,' said Jason in a hard whisper. 'I give everything back. Take it all. All of it. The bike, the skateboard, the book, the games . . . the fish. Everything in the shed.' Jason looked at Quicksilver. The skin over his cheeks was pulled taut and aching white. Jason hesitated the merest fraction of a second. 'The magic mitt. I give it back.'

Jason and Penny waited fearfully, not daring to breathe. Slowly, almost imperceptibly, the rocking motion began to subside. A faint wash of red colour rose beneath Quicksilver's skin.

Jason watched him hard, willing the colour to brighten.

'It's moving!' cried Penny.

Jason looked up. Slowly, slowly the tunnel had begun to move again. Foot by foot. Faster. Then faster. Closer and closer to its end it travelled, until finally, with a great whoosh, it burst free into the daylight again.

There was a great clap of thunder. The energy streaked upwards and seemed to explode in the air. Then it fell like rain all along Poplar Street. And all along Poplar Street, where the tunnel lay safely beneath, the pavement dissolved. Grasses and bushes grew, and elegant trees that reached towards the sky. And the tallest and most elegant of trees grew, by luck or by design, before the wide south windows of Silas Becker's house.

'Nice finish, don't you think?' said Quicksilver. 'I thought of the grass and the trees myself, you know.'

Jason and Penny turned to look at him. He was sitting quite calmly with his best smile on his face. Only in the corners of his eyes could one see the little lines of relief and weariness.

'Well done,' said Penny.

'Thank you,' said Jason.

'So long,' said Quicksilver. And was gone.

10

Jason and Penny rode their bikes through the tunnel and back again. They rode through the park and along the sidewalk in front of Spider's house and Silas Becker's house and the corner store. They found good trees for sitting under and good new trees for climbing. They climbed the old cottonwood tree itself and sat high, high up in the branches and laughed for no reason at all. When kids started arriving at the ball park for the ten o'clock baseball game, they climbed down and stood beneath the cottonwood side by side.

'I miss him,' said Jason.

'Miss who?' asked Penny.

'Quicksilver, Elster of the Third Order,' said Jason. 'I never really thought about what it would be like after he'd gone.'

'Quicksilver?' asked Penny. There was an odd look on her face. She appeared to be trying to remember something that was just a shadow in her mind. As Jason watched, even the attempt at remembering seemed to be slipping by.

'Quicksilver,' said Jason. 'Quicksilver and the magic and the trees.'

'Oh Jason, I love the cottonwood tree,' said Penny. 'It's great fun and it does make me think of all kinds of magical things, but –'

Jason looked at her hard.

'Do you remember about the tunnel?' he asked carefully.

'What? The tunnel we're standing above? What about it?'

'Nothing,' said Jason.

'I'm glad they built the tunnel instead of taking the park away. Who'd have thought Silas Becker could beat City Hall after all. That's one fight I'd like to have been in on,' said Penny.

'Yes,' said Jason. 'That's what I mean.'

Jason knew, now, what was happening. The pact was completed. The magic was over. Perhaps, he too would forget it had ever happened? He didn't want to. It was too grand, too great, too special a happening in his life to ever forget.

'Come on. We'll be late for the game,' said Penny and she began to run for the diamond.

Jason stood under the tree remembering. He took a few steps away from the tree. With each step, it seemed, the picture of Quicksilver seemed to fade in his mind. He realized he could no longer remember his exact features or the colour of his hair. Jason stopped. He did not want to forget. It was not fair, to have to forget.

'Heads up, Jason!'

The voice came high out of the tree top. There was a loud crack – the crack of a bat hitting a ball. Jason looked up and spotted the white sphere arching high through the air towards him.

Glove, catch the ball, thought Jason instinctively. Instinctively, his body responded. Without even thinking about it, Jason stepped into the exact spot where the ball would fall. He caught it safely in his old glove.

'My old glove,' said Jason under his breath. 'My old glove,' he said a little louder. 'My old glove!' he cried. 'Thank you!'

He tossed the ball high up in the air again. There was a crackle and a poof as the ball disappeared.

With a new and special feeling of excitement, Jason raced for the ball park. He did not hear the sound, very much like laughter, that raced and rushed through the leaves high up in the cottonwood tree behind him as he ran. He did not see, in the uppermost branches, the briefest glint of light — as when the sun sheers off the moving glass pane of a revolving door.

the end